Mystery in Mexico

Written by Jane West

Illustrated by Seb Camagajevac

FULL FLIGHT

Titles in Full Flight 4

Badger Publishing Limited
15 Wedgwood Gate, Pin Green Industrial Estate,
Stevenage, Hertfordshire SG1 4SU
Telephone: 01438 356907. Fax: 01438 747015
www.badger-publishing.co.uk
enquiries@badger-publishing.co.uk

Mystery in Mexico ISBN 1 84691 033 1
                   ISBN 978-1-84691-033-3

Text © Jane West 2006
Complete work © Badger Publishing Limited 2006

Series Editor: Jonny Zucker
Publisher: David Jamieson
Commissioning Editor: Carrie Lewis
Editor: Paul Martin
Design: Fiona Grant
Illustration: Seb Camagajevac

Mystery in Mexico

Contents

Midday heat

The midday sun beat down. Sam lay in her hammock. Everyone else was having a sleep – that was what they did in Mexico when the sun got too hot.

Every summer, she and her father came to this wild and lonely part of Mexico. Sam's dad was a top archaeologist in England, but what he really loved were summers spent digging around ruins in Mexico.

Sam normally enjoyed a rest at midday. She liked rocking in the giant hammock under the shade of a large tree. Today she couldn't sleep. She was wide awake.

Sam swung out of the hammock and walked off into the forest. It would be easy to get lost in the trees.

Sam checked her compass before setting off. She wasn't supposed to go far by herself, but today Sam didn't care. Something was calling to her…

6

Treasure Hunters

Voices in the forest. Sam stopped and listened. She could hear people chatting. That was good – it meant she hadn't been seen.

But above the Mexican voices, there was one loud voice that sounded American. That was bad.

There was only one person around here who spoke like that – Rafe Spinks, the slimy American archaeologist with his black Jeep and big hats.

Sam's father said he was not a real archaeologist – he only cared about finding treasure. Not only that, but he paid the local warlord José Mamexi to help him. Even the Police were afraid of Mamexi.

Her father needed to know that Spinks and Mamexi were looking close by.

Sam crept away to warn him. She looked down at her compass. It wasn't pointing north. It was spinning in a circle, not pointing at anything.

A wave of fear passed over Sam.

Lost

Sam tried to work out which way she should go. "If the sun is behind me, then the camp must be to my right."

She went back through the forest, trying to keep the sun behind her. But the weeds tripped her up and thorns stuck in her clothes. It was as if the forest didn't want to free her. Soon, she was fed up.

"I'm so stupid!" she said to herself.
"Dad always tells me to take water
with me and tell someone where I'm
going!"

But it was no good – she was lost. Sam
sat down. The third thing her Dad
always told her was to stay where she
was if she ever got lost.

Sam leaned against a large rock to think. "That's odd," she said to herself.

The rock was not like a normal stone. It had sharp edges. It looked like part of a wall.

She pulled away the plants that had grown around the sharp stone and scraped away the dirt and soil.

Soon she could see more stone. Sam
gasped. She realised that she was
looking at a stone door – one that
hadn't been opened for hundreds of
years.

Danger in the Dark

"Dad wouldn't like this," thought Sam. But she couldn't stop now. Sam pushed the door open. It moved easily, as if it wanted her to go in.

Sunshine showed her the first few steps, but then it was dark. Sam took a deep breath and stepped inside. She worked her way along, feeling the way with her fingers.

"Aagh!" Something was moving by her hand.

Sam kept walking, her eyes becoming used to the dark.

The floor started to slope downwards. "If I don't get out of here," she said to herself, "they won't even find my body!"

That was too much for Sam. She turned to go back, but at that moment she saw a light ahead of her. What on earth could it be?

She walked into a cave with a shelf cut into the back wall. It reminded Sam of the Aztec altars that she'd seen in the big museum in Mexico City.

In the centre of the shelf was a round, glass object. It seemed to glow.

As she went closer, Sam could see that the object wasn't really round, it was a skull. A skull made of pure crystal.

The Skull

"These are really, really rare," said Sam as she looked at the crystal skull.

The museum in Mexico had one and there was another one in Paris. There were more in other big museums. But they had all been found in Mexico.

Sam had heard her father and other archaeologists talking about crystal skulls. Why were they made? Some people said that the skulls must have magic powers that we did not understand.

To this day, nobody knew how the ancient Aztecs made the skulls with only simple tools.

"We just can't work out why they exist," said Sam's father, "but they do."

One archaeologist had even suggested that the skulls were made by aliens – but no-one believed him.

"I must get this to dad," said Sam. "It will be the find of his life!"
Sam reached out to pick up the skull.

"Don't touch that!"

Sam jumped at the sound of a man's voice.

Rafe Spinks stood in the cave, holding his torch like a gun.

"Leave it, girl!" he ordered. "It could be a trap. Even a kid like you should know that. Haven't you seen any Indiana Jones films?"

Next to him a short, dark-haired man giggled. "Get the skull and give me my money," he said. He sounded Mexican and he smelled bad.

"The girl is the daughter of that old English guy," said Spinks. "These archaeologists are always in my way."

"Don't worry, I'll deal with the girl."

Sam's throat went dry. She was looking right into the cold eyes of the evil warlord José Mamexi.

Warlord Worries

Spinks looked angrily at the ugly man but then he went back to the skull.

Mamexi began to walk towards Sam.

Sam cried out in alarm and backed away from him. "Help me!" she begged.

Spinks didn't move and Sam felt
Mamexi's damp hands reach for her
neck.

Suddenly a scream filled the cave.

The skull's eyes glowed with blue fire,
burning into Spinks and Mamexi.
They fell to the ground.

A feeling of calm filled Sam. The skull seemed to be telling her what to do.

She picked up the skull then ran back up to the door. The two men were still on the ground behind her.

Back in daylight, Sam ran through the forest, jumping easily over fallen trees and vines.

She arrived in the camp out of breath and fell into her father's arms.

"Where have you been?" he cried. "I was so worried!"

"Dad, look!" said Sam. "Look what I've found!"

The archaeologists gathered round, staring in silence at the crystal skull.

"Where did you find it?" asked her father in a voice that shook.

"In the forest," said Sam. "Spinks and Mamexi were there, too."

Her father looked up in alarm. "Did they hurt you?" he asked.

"I think they might have," said Sam, "but the skull saved me."

"What do you mean?" asked her father, confused.

"I don't know," whispered Sam. Mamexi tried to grab me and… and… I don't know. The skull just lit up and it hurt them. It made them scream. It wanted to help me… and it wanted *me* to help *it*. The skull said it wanted to see sunlight again. And… and… that's it."

Her father stared at her in silence.

"I know it sounds crazy," said Sam. "But that's what happened."

She looked at the crystal skull. But the skull was still and lifeless, gleaming under the Mexican sunshine. It was happy to keep its secrets – for now.